Classic Children's Tales

RANDOLPH CALDECOTT · EDWARD LEAR · KATE GREENAWAY · BEATRIX POTTER

150 Years
of Frederick Warne

Classic Children's Tales

RANDOLPH CALDECOTT
EDWARD LEAR
KATE GREENAWAY
BEATRIX POTTER

150 YEARS
of FREDERICK WARNE

FREDERICK WARNE
UK | USA | Canada | Ireland | Australia
India | New Zealand | South Africa

Frederick Warne is part of the Penguin Random House group of companies
whose addresses can be found at global.penguinrandomhouse.com.

First published in 2015
The Sly Old Cat first published in 1971
001

Printed in China

A catalogue record for this book is available from the British Library

ISBN 978-0-2411-9871-1

CONTENTS

PUBLISHER'S FOREWORD

The publishing house of Warne was begun in London in 1865 and grew quickly, establishing an office in New York in 1881. From the very beginning, Warne was a pioneer in children's books and colour picture books in particular, publishing many of the greatest authors and illustrators at a time when few publishers strayed into the children's market.

2015 marks the 150th anniversary of Frederick Warne and Company and, to celebrate, we have collected here works by four of the most prestigious authors and illustrators originally published by Warne. Kate Greenaway, Randolph Caldecott, Edward Lear, and Beatrix Potter produced some of the most beautiful, witty, and successful children's books of the last century and a half, which have been enjoyed by children all around the world.

The works included in this collection range from well-known classics such as Greenaway's *Mother Goose* and Lear's *Book of Nonsense*, which revolutionised picture-book illustration and limericks respectively, to lesser-known delights such as Caldecott's *Sing a Song for Sixpence*. A rarely-seen story by Beatrix Potter, *The Sly Old Cat*, is also included. Begun towards the end of her writing career, when Potter's eyesight was failing, the illustrations were never completed and the book was only published after her death.

The influence of each of these authors and illustrators is still felt today. Kate Greenaway and Randolph Caldecott lent their names to medals awarded to the artist of the most distinguished children's picture books in the United Kingdom and United States respectively. The works of all four have reached classic status and are popular around the world.

Each section is introduced by a successful and current author or illustrator, who each give a unique insight into the continued importance of these classic books for children.

Over the years Frederick Warne has continued to publish important and beloved books for children, from Eric Hill's classic Spot stories to Cicely Mary Barker's beautiful and delicate Flower Fairies. In 1983 Warne was acquired by Penguin Books where it continues as an imprint today. Warne remains the official publisher of Beatrix Potter, having published the first trade edition of *The Tale of Peter Rabbit*, and all of Potter's subsequent titles.

This collection brings together some of the most truly classic children's books, reproduced as they would have first appeared and published by Warne once again. It is a fitting tribute and celebration of one hundred and fifty years of Frederick Warne and Company.

BEATRIX
POTTER

BEATRIX POTTER

As a child, I was a reluctant reader: so many of the books I was given to read I found condescending. But I never felt that way about Beatrix Potter. My earliest memories are of looking through her books and wondering at the pictures. My first Potter, which I have beside me now on my desk, is a copy of *The Tale of Mr. Tod*, which I appear to have "permanently borrowed" from Blackheath High School (with no apologies!). What an irresistible blend of injured pride and utter peril there is in that book. Potter's writing is pure joy for a young and curious mind: her books taught me how to enjoy reading.

I strongly believe that Beatrix Potter never put her childhood "away". She would call on that wonder and sharp-focused observation and give it straight back to the young reader, along with a wonderful sprinkling of sophisticated humour and wry observations of fickle and funny human nature laid bare.

Beatrix Potter was an extraordinary woman, with an acute sense of self and a determination to learn and observe that stayed with her from her childhood, where she spent summers in the rugged nature of Scotland as well as in the cultured drawing rooms of London.

Beatrix Potter was an extraordinary and pioneering woman who used her incredible talents to explore her world, to draw it, write it, and give it back to us.

So here's to Beatrix: artist, scientist, author, sheep farmer, loyal wife, and keen mind.

Eleanor Taylor

Eleanor Taylor is the illustrator of three further tales about Peter Rabbit, written by Emma Thompson and published by Frederick Warne.

The first edition of
The Sly Old Cat

THE SLY OLD CAT

Written and illustrated
by Beatrix Potter

This is a sly old Cat, who gave
a tea-party to a rat.

This is the rat in his best
clothes coming down the area
steps. They had their tea in
the kitchen.

"How do you do? Mr. Rat!
Will you sit on this chair?"
said the Cat.

"I will eat *my* bread and
butter first," said the Cat,
"and then *you* shall eat the
crumbs that are left, Mr. Rat!"

"This is a very rude way of
treating visitors!" said Mr.
Rat to himself.

"Now I will pour out *my* tea,"
said the Cat, "and you shall
lick up the drops that are left
in the milk jug, Mr. Rat; and
then *I* will have some dessert!"
said the Cat.

"I believe she is going to eat
me for dessert; I wish I'd
never come!" said poor
Mr. Rat.

She tipped up the milk jug –
that greedy old Cat! she
didn't want to leave one single
drop for the rat.

But the rat jumped on the
table and gave the jug a pat,
and it slipped down quite
tight over the head of the Cat!

Then the Cat banged about
the kitchen with its head fast
in the jug,

and the rat sat on the table
drinking tea out of a mug.

Then he put a muffin in a
paper bag and went away.

And he ate the whole muffin at
one sitting; so that is the end
of the Rat.

March 20th 06.

And the Cat broke the jug
against the leg of the kitchen
table; so that is the end of
the Cat.

RANDOLPH
CALDECOTT

RANDOLPH CALDECOTT

When the Randolph Caldecott Medal was first awarded in 1938 by the American Library Association, the name "Caldecott" brought attention and luster to the new award. Long after the British artist's death in 1886, his series of sixteen picture books based on nursery rhymes, songs, and comic poems were a staple on the bookshelves of children throughout the English-speaking world.

The books may not be as universally known today, yet their influence in picture books is everywhere. Whenever you see an illustrated book in which an extended action deploys across multiple pages; whenever you turn a page and pause on a spread with no words at all, you're seeing tropes that were new with Caldecott. Whenever you find slyly planted clues in the pictures that suggest subplots not apparent in the text, that is Caldecott. Before movies, his books were cinematic.

So here is the original. In this selection, note how the song's changed title, "Sing a Song *for* (not "of") Sixpence," in conjunction with the frontispiece [see overleaf], launches a story: it explains how this one child willing to sing for an elderly lady will receive the coin that starts the plot rolling: given in charity to a woodcutter, sixpence buys the rye that traps the birds that go in the pie. . . . And what a charming idea to make the king and queen children themselves! What does it mean? The more you study the pictures, the more ideas you may get.

Maurice Sendak, a great champion of the artist, said, simply, "Caldecott did it best."

Paul O. Zelinsky

Among many other awards and prizes, Paul O. Zelinsky received the 1998 Caldecott Medal for his retelling of Rapunzel, as well as Caldecott Honours for three of his books: Hansel and Gretel *(1983),* Rumpelstiltskin *(1987), and* Swamp Angel *(1995).*

An early edition of Sing a Song for Sixpence

SING A SONG
FOR SIXPENCE

Illustrated by
Randolph Caldecott

SING A SONG FOR SIXPENCE

Sing a Song for Sixpence,

A Pocketful of Rye;

Sing a Song for Sixpence

Four-and-Twenty Blackbirds

Baked

in a Pie.

Sing a Song for Sixpence

When the Pie was opened,
The Birds began to sing;

Was not that

a dainty Dish

To set before the King?

The King was in

his Counting-house,

Counting out his Money.

The Queen was in

the Parlour,

Eating Bread and Honey.

The Maid was in

the Garden,

Hanging out the Clothes;

There came a little Blackbird,

And snapped off her Nose.

But there came a
Jenny Wren
and popped it on again.

KATE GREENAWAY

KATE GREENAWAY

My first sighting of Kate's lovely pictures was in the library of Mrs. Chambers, my first art teacher at Leominster, Herefordshire, during the summer of '46. There weren't any picture books in the shops in those days - so seeing these delightful images and being able to handle them was the equivalent to me of being in Aladdin's cave.

I had been brought up in the West of Poland (then annexed to the German Reich). The Nazis did not allow the sale of Polish books but I had access to my grandmother's library which, oddly enough, comprised Kipling's star characters – Mowgli and Stalky were my favourites. I would climb a tree and read them in Polish translation. They had no pictures – the pictures were in my mind, but they gave me a fascinating glimpse into a faraway animal kingdom. Stalky & Co. was more mysterious but gave me some idea of an English boys' school. I little knew I was destined to end up in an English public school the following year.

But it was at Cambridge that I was able to study in depth and more detail Kate Greenaway's brilliant pictures in the privacy of the University Library, without the constant interruptions that my college library inexorably provided. I realised what a tremendous breakthrough Kate had achieved. No woman had attained such a high profile as an illustrator nor indeed done better drawings of young people in a completely imagined world. It was perhaps then it dawned on me that if she could succeed against all the odds, perhaps I could have a go. After all an illustrator doesn't have to speak the language from birth!

Jan Pieńkowski

Born in Poland in 1936, Jan Pieńkowski is a celebrated illustrator of children's books, including the Meg and Mog series, and has twice won the Kate Greenaway medal.

Early editions of A Apple Pie *and* Mother Goose

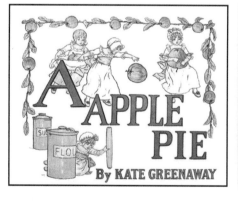

Publisher's note: Please be aware that the letter *I* does not appear in this traditional rhyme as, when first composed, no distinction was made between the written forms of *I* and *J*

An extract from

A APPLE PIE

By Kate Greenaway

A Apple Pie

A APPLE PIE

B BIT IT

C CUT IT

D DEALT IT

A Apple Pie

E EAT IT

KG

F FOUGHT FOR IT

G GOT IT

H HAD IT

J JUMPED FOR IT

K KNELT FOR IT

L LONGED FOR IT

M MOURNED FOR IT

Mother Goose
or the
Old Nursery Rhymes

Illustrated by
· Kate Greenaway ·

LONDON
FREDERICK WARNE
AND NEW YORK

A selection from
MOTHER GOOSE

Illustrated by
Kate Greenaway

Little Jack Horner sat in the corner,
    Eating a Christmas pie ;
He put in his thumb, and pulled out a plum,
    And said, oh ! what a good boy am I.

Jack Sprat could eat no fat,
His wife could eat no lean;
And so between them both,
They licked the platter clean.

Mother Goose

Jack and Jill
Went up the hill,
To fetch a pail of water ;
Jack fell down
And broke his crown,
And Jill came tumbling after.

Little Bo-peep has lost her sheep,
And can't tell where to find them ;
Leave them alone, and they'll come home.
And bring their tails behind them.

Mother Goose

Polly put the kettle on
Polly put the kettle on,
Polly put the kettle on,
We'll all have tea.
Sukey take it off again,
Sukey take it off again,
Sukey take it off again,
They're all gone away.

Mary, Mary, quite contrary,
How does your garden grow ?
With silver bells, and cockle shells,
And cowslips all of a row.

Mother Goose

Billy boy blue, come blow me your horn,
The sheep's in the meadow, the cow's
in the corn ;
Is that the way you mind your sheep,
Under the haycock fast asleep !

Girls and boys come out to play,
The moon it shines as bright as day ;
Leave your supper, and leave your sleep,
And come to your playmates in the street ;
Come with a whoop, come with a call.
Come with a good will, or come not at all ;
Up the ladder and down the wall,
A halfpenny loaf will serve us all.

Rock-a-bye baby,
Thy cradle is green ;
Father's a nobleman,
Mother's a queen.
And Betty's a lady,
And wears a gold ring ;
And Johnny's a drummer,
And drums for the king.

Little Miss Muffet,
Sat on a tuffet,
Eating some curds and whey ;
There came a great spider,
And sat down beside her,
And frightened Miss Muffet away.

Humpty Dumpty sat on a wall,
Humpty Dumpty had a great fall.

K.G.

Ring-a-ring-a-roses,
A pocket full of posies ;
Hush ! hush ! hush ! hush !
We're all tumbled down.

EDWARD LEAR

EDWARD LEAR

"How pleasant to know Mr. Lear! Who has written such volumes of stuff!"

Though he said it himself in 1879, these lines from an eight-stanza verse he wrote state how readers of all ages have been and will continue to be amused by Lear's clever, timeless volumes of stuff!

It is, indeed, pleasant to know Mr. Lear via this sampling of his classic verses, songs, limericks, and artwork. Each time I read something he has written I smile again or chalk up another hearty laugh. His wit is contagious.

Born 1812, in England, Lear was the twentieth child of Jeremiah Lear, a London stockbroker, and his wife, Ann. Although young Lear was able to make a living drawing at the age of fifteen, his first book, *The Book of Nonsense*, a collection of limericks and drawings appeared when he was thirty-four years old.

In 1871 "The Owl and the Pussy-Cat" was published in *Nonsense Songs, Stories, Botany and Alphabets*, instantly becoming a favorite verse. It remains one of the most popular beloved poems ever written for children.

"How charmingly sweet you sing!" said Pussy-Cat to Owl. We can all sing praise to Mr. Lear for the fun-filled limericks, his wondrous made-up words, his songs and drawings that continue to live on and on and on.

Lee Bennett Hopkins

Lee Bennett Hopkins is recognised as "the world's most prolific anthologist of poetry for children" by Guinness World Records. His many honors include the NCTE Award for Excellence in Poetry for Children. He lives in Cape Coral, Florida.

Early editions of Nonsense Songs and Stories *and The Book of Nonsense*

A selection from
NONSENSE
SONGS & STORIES

By Edward Lear

THE OWL AND THE PUSSY-CAT

I.

THE Owl and the Pussy-Cat went to sea
In a beautiful pea-green boat,
They took some honey, and plenty of money,
Wrapped up in a five-pound note.
The Owl looked up to the stars above,
And sang to a small guitar,
" O lovely Pussy ! O Pussy, my love,
What a beautiful Pussy you are,
You are,
You are !
What a beautiful Pussy you are !"

II.

Pussy said to the Owl, " You elegant fowl !
How charmingly sweet you sing !
O let us be married ! too long we have tarried :
But what shall we do for a ring ?"
They sailed away for a year and a day,
To the land where the Bong-tree grows,
And there in a wood a Piggy-wig stood,
With a ring at the end of his nose,
His nose,
His nose,
With a ring at the end of his nose.

III.

"Dear Pig, are you willing to sell for one shilling
Your ring ?" Said the Piggy, "I will."
So they took it away, and were married next day
By the Turkey who lives on the hill.

They dined on mince, and slices of quince,
Which they ate with a runcible spoon ;
And hand in hand, on the edge of the sand,
They danced by the light of the moon,
The moon,
The moon,
They danced by the light of the moon.

THE JUMBLIES

I.

THEY went to sea in a Sieve, they did,
In a Sieve they went to sea :
In spite of all their friends could say,
On a winter's morn, on a stormy day,
In a Sieve they went to sea !
And when the Sieve turned round and round,
And every one cried, " You'll all be drowned !"
They called aloud, " Our Sieve ain't big,
But we don't care a button ! we don't care a fig !
In a Sieve we'll go to sea ! "
Far and few, far and few,
Are the lands where the Jumblies live ;

Their heads are green, and their hands are blue,
And they went to sea in a Sieve.

II.
They sailed away in a Sieve, they did,
In a Sieve they sailed so fast,
With only a beautiful pea-green veil
Tied with a riband by way of a sail,
To a small tobacco-pipe mast ;
And every one said, who saw them go,
"O won't they be soon upset, you know !
For the sky is dark, and the voyage is long,
And happen what may, it's extremely wrong
In a Sieve to sail so fast ! "
Far and few, far and few,
Are the lands where the Jumblies live ;
Their heads are green, and their hands are blue,
And they went to sea in a Sieve.

III.
The water it soon came in, it did,
The water it soon came in ;
So to keep them dry, they wrapped their feet
In a pinky paper all folded neat,
And they fastened it down with a pin.
And they passed the night in a crockery-jar,
And each of them said, " How wise we are !

Though the sky be dark, and the voyage be long,
Yet we never can think we were rash or wrong,
While round in our Sieve we spin ! ”
Far and few, far and few,
Are the lands where the Jumblies live ;
Their heads are green, and their hands are blue,
And they went to sea in a Sieve.

IV.

And all night long they sailed away ;
And when the sun went down,
They whistled and warbled a moony song
To the echoing sound of a coppery gong,
In the shade of the mountains brown.
“O Timballo ! How happy we are,
When we live in a sieve and a crockery-jar,
And all night long in the moonlight pale,
We sail away with a pea-green sail,
In the shade of the mountains brown ! ”
Far and few, far and few,
Are the lands where the Jumblies live ;
Their heads are green, and their hands are blue,
And they went to sea in a Sieve.

V.

They sailed to the Western Sea, they did,
To a land all covered with trees,

And they bought an Owl, and a useful Cart,
And a pound of Rice, and a Cranberry Tart,
And a hive of silvery Bees.
And they bought a Pig, and some green Jack-daws,
And a lovely Monkey with lollipop paws,
And forty bottles of Ring-Bo-Ree,
And no end of Stilton Cheese.
Far and few, far and few,
Are the lands where the Jumblies live ;
Their heads are green, and their hands are blue,
And they went to sea in a Sieve.

VI.

And in twenty years they all came back,
In twenty years or more,
And every one said, " How tall they've grown !
For they've been to the Lakes, and the Terrible Zone,
And the hills of the Chankly Bore ; "
And they drank their health, and gave them a feast
Of dumplings made of beautiful yeast ;
And every one said, " If we only live,
We too will go to sea in a Sieve,—
To the hills of the Chankly Bore ! "
Far and few, far and few,
Are the lands where the Jumblies live ;
Their heads are green, and their hands are blue,
And they went to sea in a Sieve.

THE YONGHY BONGHY BO.

On the coast of Co – ro – man-del, Where the ear – ly pumpkins grow, In the

middle of the woods, Lived the Yonghy Bonghy Bò; Two old chairs and half a candle, One old

jug with-out a han-dle; These were all his worldly goods, In the middle of the woods, These were

all the world-ly goods, Of the Yong-hy Bong-hy Bò, Of the Yong-hy Bong-hy Bò.

A selection from
THE BOOK
OF NONSENSE

By Edward Lear

There was an Old Man with a beard,
who said, " It is just as I feared !—
Two Owls and a Hen, four Larks and a Wren,
Have all built their nests in my beard ! "

There was a Young Lady whose chin
resembled the point of a pin ;
So she had it made sharp, and purchased a harp,
And played several tunes with her chin.

There was a Young Lady of Dorking,
who bought a large bonnet for walking ;
But its colour and size so bedazzled her eyes,
That she very soon went back to Dorking.

There was an Old Man of the West,
who wore a pale plum-coloured vest ;
When they said, "Does it fit ?" he replied, " Not a bit ! "
That uneasy Old Man of the West.

There was an Old Person of Dutton,
whose head was as small as a button;
So, to make it look big, he purchased a wig,
And rapidly rushed about Dutton.

There was an Old Person of Gretna,
who rushed down the crater of Etna ;
When they said, " Is it hot ? " he replied, " No, it's not ! "
That mendacious Old Person of Gretna.

There was an Old Man on whose nose,
   most birds of the air could repose ;
But they all flew away at the closing of day,
Which relieved that Old Man and his nose.

There was an Old Man of Aosta,
who possessed a large cow, but he lost her ;
But they said, " Don't you see she has rushed up a tree ?
You invidious Old Man of Aosta ! "

THE END